Little Zebra

written by Jay Dale

illustrated by Jacqueline East

Little Zebra went
into the jungle.

"Look at that elephant,"
he said to Mum.
"I can see an elephant
looking at me!"

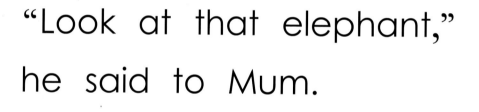

"Little Zebra," said Mum.
"That elephant is **not** looking
at you."

Little Zebra went
into the grass.

"Look at that ant,"
he said to Mum.
"I can see an ant
looking at me!"

6

"Little Zebra," said Mum.
"That ant is **not** looking
at you."

Little Zebra went into the river.

"Look at that crocodile,"
he said to Mum.
"I can see a crocodile
looking at me!"

"Little Zebra," said Mum.
"That crocodile **is** looking
at you!"

15

"Run, Little Zebra! Run!" shouted Mum.